Desert Letters

by David Neufeld
illustrated by Leslie Bowman

Harcourt

Orlando Boston Dallas Chicago San Diego

Visit *The Learning Site!*

www.harcourtschool.com

Furnace Creek, California, February 18, 2001

Dear Bud,

I'd heard about Badwater and Death Valley. I never thought I'd visit them. Badwater, California, is the lowest point in the United States. The water is bad, really BAD. It has all kinds of salts in it. It would pickle your tongue if you ever tasted it. Uncle Mert got down and looked into the water with a scope. Uncle Mert is a science nut. He said enthusiastically, "There are things living in that water!" He also pointed to a thin plant and said, "Pickle weed."

That water could pickle anything. Not much is alive here. Well, Uncle Mert, Aunt Carla, my cousin Rick, and I are alive. Rick said we're 282 feet below sea level. I don't know why he had to tell me. The park sign says that. Rick also said that it's lucky we came in February. Apparently, it gets to be 130 degrees here in July! Rick looked at me and said, "The spot you're standing on is transformed into a frying pan."

I don't think Uncle Mert would bring us here in July.

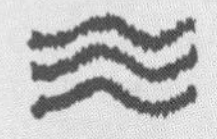

I walked on the rough salt beds. Up close, the salt beds look like razor-sharp mountains. Some of the crystals are a foot tall. A crow flew down and landed near me. It stepped along the salt as if it hurt to walk there. I think the crow was hungry. I watched it fly off. It disappeared into the tops of the Funeral Mountains. Everything here in Death Valley has a strange name. Tonight we're camping at Furnace Creek. Maybe I'll try to find Dead Man's Gulch. That would be great. At night it is really cool here.

Your pal,

Luke

NEVADA
UTAH
Furnace Creek
Death Valley
Mojave Desert
ARIZONA
CALIFORNIA
Needles
Lake Havasu
N
W
E
S

Furnace Creek, CA, February 19, 2001

Dear Bud,

Uncle Mert's trailer looks funny. We're in the desert, right? He has a boat on the trailer. Uncle Mert says, "Just in case." There's not a cloud in the sky. The park guide said that a quarter inch of rain fell three weeks ago. He said that was a lot.

Aunt Carla took Rick and me to investigate a wash. That means a shallow canyon made by water. It's hard to imagine where enough water would come from to carve the wash. Aunt Carla says the desert gets flash floods. I can't imagine that.

Aunt Carla pointed to some rabbit brush, and a rabbit jumped out! Then Rick pointed to a hole in the side of the wash. He said it was a bird's nest. Nothing came out.

The wonderful part came when we climbed out of the wash. The desert was covered with flowers! Aunt Carla called the smallest ones belly flowers. She said you have to get on your belly to see them.

There were also taller flowers. They looked like the ones your mom grows. Rick said seeds may wait thirty years for rain. Then they start to grow. These desert flowers may live only for a few weeks. They grow and their flowers bloom. Then they make seeds for new flowers and die. Not a very long life, is it?

When we got back, Uncle Mert was packed up. We're going to Barstow.

Got a lot of snow?

See you,

Luke

Barstow, California, February 21, 2001

Dear Bud,

We took all yesterday to get here. Barstow is a truck-stop town. It has a kind of strange décor.

Aunt Carla wanted to look for creosote bushes. Uncle Mert came to find mice and coyotes. Rick went with Aunt Carla. I chose to search for the mice and coyotes. I walked into the desert with Uncle Mert. Both of us carried camera stuff. I had no idea where we would find mice in the desert. I wasn't sure I wanted to find a coyote.

We did find creosote bushes. They grow as if they were planted a certain distance apart. Uncle Mert told me why. Each bush makes a poison that keeps other creosote bushes from growing too close. The roots go down 100 feet to get water!

When we got a half a mile from the campground, Mert stopped. He put down his bag. He took the tripod out and set it up. I got the flash stuff from my bag. Mert had two cameras with shutter cables. We put a thin wire in a square about 20 feet to a side. This would be the trip wire for a coyote.

Mert connected the trip wire to the shutter cable on one camera. He set up the other camera to take pictures every ten minutes. It would click for three hours starting at midnight. We left a note on the cameras. We explained that it was a science experiment. The note also said "Please don't touch." The note was for people. We hoped the coyotes couldn't read.

That night the four of us sat around outside until late. Twice we saw the flash go off. Rick fell asleep. I'm glad I came here.

Your pal,

Luke

Mailbox, Mojave Desert, CA, February 22, 2001

Dear Bud,

We don't spend much time in the trailer. It's used mostly for cooking. It's also good to put stuff in. We sleep in tents or under the stars since it never rains.

All four of us went to get the cameras this morning. Mert downloaded the pictures onto his laptop. We all bent over the screen to look. There were fourteen pictures of mice. I mean LOTS of mice, running around. The trip wire caught pictures of two coyotes and one fox. In one, a coyote had caught a mouse.

I hope they pick up mail here,
Luke

Lake Havasu, Arizona, February 23, 2001

Dear Bud,

We stopped in Needles for food and other things. Then we went on to Lake Havasu Wildlife Reserve. All of a sudden the desert opened up. There was the Colorado River. There were dams all along the river. It was more like a long lake.

It was afternoon by the time we got the food and everything in the boat. Then we got the boat into the water. Right off, I saw an eagle, my first ever! Rick, of course, has seen lots of them. He says spotting a bighorn sheep is the real test. I guess they're shy. They're also not in the water.

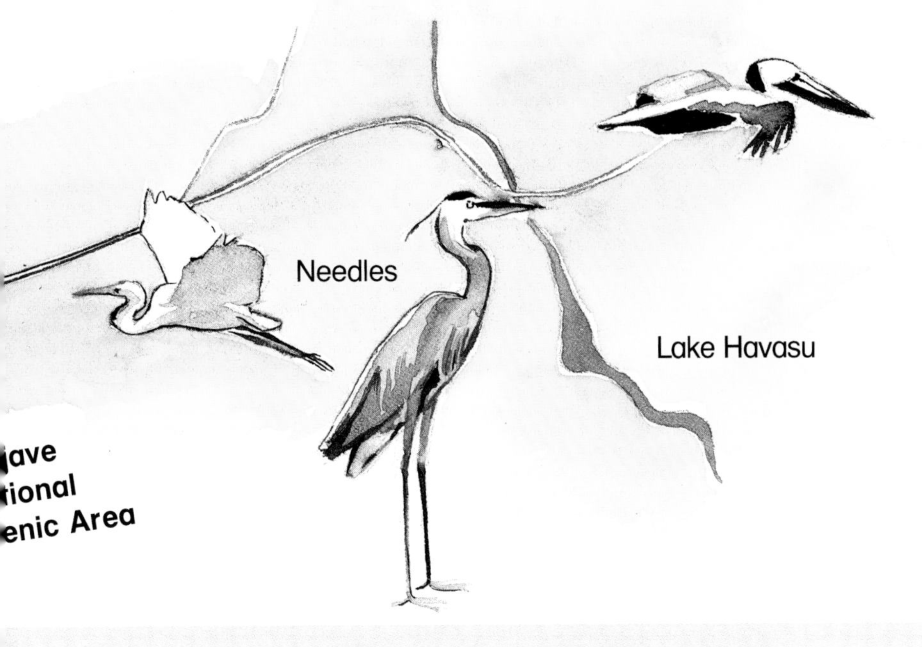

Uncle Mert rowed us around Topnock Marsh. Aunt Carla pointed out the different water birds. You should have seen the sunset! It was like red and yellow paints stretched across the sky.

Needles, CA, February 27, 2001

Dear Bud,

We are back in Needles after a real scare! It happened three days ago. Uncle Mert wanted to move the trailer to a quiet place. We followed a dirt road through a bunch of washes. They were like the washes in Death Valley. A sign along the dirt road said "Flash Flood Corridor."

The road ahead of us looked bad. Uncle Mert didn't think he could make it any farther. He tried to turn around in a wide part of the wash. We got stuck. He unhitched the truck, and we got it out of the wash. The trailer was left behind. Uncle Mert said the rangers come through every evening. They'd help us get it out of there. So we had breakfast and walked around. I saw bobcat prints in the wash. Later the sky got hazy. Uncle Mert and Aunt Carla went to explore the wash.

Rick and I found a deck of cards in the trailer. I wanted to play Hearts, but Rick wanted to play War. We played War.

Rick and I were at war four times in a row. The cards hardly fit on the little table. I heard raindrops on the roof. The table shook. Then the cards started falling.

"Earthquake?" I asked.

We climbed out of the trailer. The sky to the east was dark. I mean DARK. Then we saw the water about a mile away. It was rushing toward us. We looked for my aunt and uncle. We saw the tops of their heads a hundred yards below us.

"MERT!" I yelled. They started climbing up the bank.

I closed the trailer door and started running out of the wash. We were going to lose the trailer! Too bad!

Rick was already standing by the truck. Mert and Carla rushed up to him. They had made it! "Come on, Luke!" they yelled. I was running and climbing.

"WHAM!" The first stones and water hit the trailer and pushed it down the wash. We all watched it float toward the Colorado River.

We groaned and then cheered when the trailer got caught. It was between two boulders. We slapped each other on the back and hugged when we saw the water level go down. "You closed the trailer door," Rick said. "You made it float!"

I guess I did!

Can't wait to tell you more,

Luke